QUE

MAULED BY A BEAR

Sue Hamilton

VISIT US AT

WWW.ABDOPUBLISHING.COM

Published by ABDO Publishing Company, 8000 West 78th Street, Suite 310, Edina, MN 55439. Copyright ©2010 by Abdo Consulting Group, Inc. International copyrights reserved in all countries. No part of this book may be reproduced in any form without written permission from the publisher. ABDO & Daughters™ is a trademark and logo of ABDO Publishing Company.

Printed in the United States of America, North Mankato, Minnesota
112009
012010

 PRINTED ON RECYCLED PAPER

Editor & Graphic Design: John Hamilton
Cover Design: John Hamilton
Cover Photo: iStockphoto
Interior Photos and Illustrations: AP Images, p. 12, 16, 21; Corbis, p. 4; Getty Images, p. 7, 18, 22, 23, 26, 27, 28, 29; iStockphoto, p. 1, 6, 8, 9, 11, 15, 17, 25, 32; Jupiter Images, p. 3, 8; David Olson, p. 5, 10, 13, 14; Photo Researchers, p. 8, 19, 20, 24.

Library of Congress Cataloging-in-Publication Data

Hamilton, Sue L., 1959-
  Mauled by a bear / Sue Hamilton.
      p. cm. -- (Close encounters of the wild kind)
  Includes index.
  ISBN 978-1-60453-932-5
  1. Bear attacks--Juvenile literature. I. Title.
  QL737.C27H3593 2010
  599.78'168--dc22
                          2009035078

CONTENTS

BEARS OUT THERE

Bears are designed by nature to rule their world. They have excellent hearing and a keen sense of smell. Their powerful jaws are filled with large, sharp teeth. Strong, muscle-bound legs end in nonretractable claws. And even though bears range in size from an American black bear's 200 pounds (91 kg) to a polar bear's whopping 1,000 pounds (454 kg), these animals are fast. Bears can run up to 35 miles per hour (56 kph), fast enough even to catch Olympic gold medalist sprinter Usain Bolt.

Adult bears have no natural enemies—except for humans. In the United States, bears are found in 42 of the 50 states. As human cities expand into bear habitats, people are increasingly finding themselves face-to-face with these leaders of the animal kingdom.

Right: A brown bear runs through a stream while fishing for salmon in Alaska.

> **"Sometimes you eat the bear. Sometimes the bear eats you."**
> —Proverb explaining the meaning of life

A person is far more likely to be struck by lightning than to be killed by a bear. Most bears prefer to stay away from people. But encounters happen. And when bears feel threatened or hungry, they do what instinct tells them to do: they attack.

An unarmed person who faces a wild bear is in grave danger. Humans are no match for these powerful predators. Some people become grisly additions to the short list of bear attack victims. Others beat the odds, surviving to tell their horrifying tales of being mauled by a bear.

Above: A polar bear hunting for prey in northern Canada, near the Arctic Circle.
Facing page: A grizzly bear in Montana.

MUSCLE, CLAWS, TEETH

There are eight different bear species: Asiatic black bear, brown bear (including grizzly and kodiac), North American black bear, panda bear, polar bear, sloth bear, spectacled bear, and sun bear. Bears are armed with claws and teeth and the muscle power to use them. A bear-to-human encounter can be a life-or-death situation.

Asiatic Black Bear   Brown Bear   North American Black Bear   Panda Bear

Polar Bear   Sloth Bear   Spectacled Bear   Sun Bear

Most bears are omnivores. They eat both plants and animals. What may be surprising to people is that most forest-living bears eat more roots, berries, nuts, and grass than they do meat. Their bodies have adapted to gathering vegetation. Their front legs are covered in muscle, ending in wide paws with 3- to 4-inch (8- to 10-cm) long claws. Digging up tasty treats in the ground is easy with these tools. But surprised bears can also use their long claws with ferocious efficiency on people.

Above: A close-up view of a grizzly bear's paws, clearly showing its sharp claws and the bottom of one paw. Photo taken in British Columbia, Canada.

Bears have 42 teeth, including four long canine teeth. Polar bears, who eat mostly fish, seal, walrus, and whale meat, have longer and sharper teeth than their forest-dwelling, vegetable-eating cousins. A polar bear's long fangs are used to grab and hold prey, as well as rip open tough hides and tear off pieces of meat. Polar bears are the biggest bears, and the most dangerous. While a seal or walrus may be fast enough and lucky enough to escape a polar bear, an unprotected, unarmed human who startles this massive white beast will probably not get away.

Black and grizzly bears have long canine teeth and sharp incisors in front, but flat molars in back. The molars allow the bears to grind up the plants they eat into small pieces. To accomplish this chewing process, bears have built up strong muscles in their jaws. And these strong muscles mean that these bears can bite hard.

Above: A bear uses its claws to help it munch down on a piece of meat.
Facing page: A black bear skull, clearly showing its large teeth.

BLACK BEAR SURPRISE

Minnesota has about 20,000 black bears living in the state. Most of these bears keep to themselves. It's rare to have a violent encounter, let alone be attacked in one's own home. However, around 9:30 pm on a fall evening in 2003, Kim Heil-Smith of Cook County opened the door from her house to her attached garage and came face-to-face with a mama bear and her cub.

With the main garage door open, the bears had entered seeking food from the garbage cans and the sunflower seeds stored inside. Heil-Smith, who was home alone but on a cell phone at the time, began yelling. She didn't want her friend to think it was another person attacking her, so she said, "It's only a bear." But the homeowner soon discovered it wasn't "only a bear," but a sow that felt trapped and wanted to protect her baby.

Above: Kim Heil-Smith in the entryway of her home, where she was attacked by a bear.

> "I tried to shut the door on her, but she was too strong. She wrapped her arms around me and I fell back."
>
> —Kim Heil-Smith, September 16, 2003, Cook County, MN

The bear attacked, biting and scratching Heil-Smith on her head, shoulder, chest, and legs. Although frightened, Heil-Smith fought back. "I just got mad at this bear being in my house. I finally was able to get my knee up so she couldn't bite me, and then I grabbed her nose and yelled, 'Get out of my house!'" Startled, the bear and her cub quickly left.

Bear experts agree that most black bears would much rather turn and run away. However, if a bear feels cornered, it will use its powerful teeth and claws to protect itself and its young.

After the attack, Heil-Smith cleaned up her own blood so family members wouldn't see it. She received medical care, and quickly forgave the bear. "I don't blame her, really; she was just protecting her baby," said Heil-Smith. But she vowed to keep her garage door closed from now on.

Above: A black bear and her cubs in their den.

GRIZZLY BEAR ATTACKS

Grizzly bears are big, fierce, and unpredictable. Their distinctive hump is a mass of muscle, which powers their forelegs. They are found from Alaska, through western Canada, and into the northwestern United States. In the lower 48 states, Montana has the most grizzlies. Listed as a threatened species for many years, studies estimate a population of less than 1,000 of the powerful predators in the state. However, human and grizzly encounters do occur. They are often terrifying, and sometimes fatal.

Above: A grizzly bear in Alaska's Denali National Park.

"I thought the whole time, 'This is so messed up. I'm going to die. I'm going to die.'"

—Roman Morris, October 6, 2007, Gardiner, Montana

College student and football player Roman Morris, along with his brother and a friend, set out on an elk hunting trip early on a Saturday morning in October 2007. The group drove to the Beattie Gulch area, just north of Gardiner, Montana. Once there, they separated.

Armed with bow and arrows, Morris settled into a spot on a hill behind some brush. He heard rustling. He put an arrow in his bow and waited quietly. However, what came out of the bushes was not an elk, but a mother grizzly bear with three cubs. He hoped it would just move away, but the bear got within a few yards of the 21-year-old and attacked.

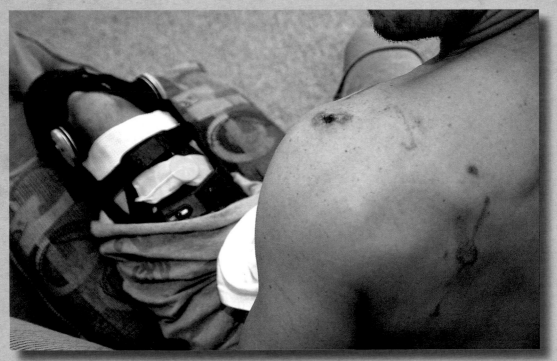

Above: Roman Morris recuperates after being mauled by a grizzly bear.

"It charged down the hill and just drilled me," said Morris. The football player fought back, punching the bear in the head. However, even at 6 feet 2 inches tall and 205 pounds (1.9 m and 93 kg), Morris was about half the size of the bear. "I put everything I had into it. It didn't budge at all."

The grizzly started clawing and biting. The sow bit his head, but Morris had on a slicker with a hood. The jacket's slippery material made the bear's jaws slip off. Still, the attack continued. The mad mother bear effortlessly tossed the athlete in the air repeatedly. She clawed him, leaving a 2-inch (5-cm) hole in the man's shoulder and a 9-inch (23-cm) gash on his leg.

Morris was sure he was dead. But then, drawn by the noise, help arrived. His friend had a pistol, and fired a shot. The bear took off. Aided by his brother and their friend, Morris made the one-mile (1.6-km) hike back to their vehicle, and then to the hospital. Lucky to be alive, Morris knows the bear was protecting her cubs. Still, Morris stated, "It was looking at me like I was an easy meal."

Above: A grizzly bear, clearly showing its distinctive hump.

"I went bald very, very suddenly."

—Johan Otter, August 25, 2005, Glacier National Park, MT

Johan Otter and his 18-year-old daughter Jenna were hiking the beautiful Grinnell Glacier Trail in Montana's Glacier National Park on a Thursday morning in August 2005. Jenna was walking in front. Suddenly, she rounded a blind corner and stopped short, muttering, "Oh, no." Johan, who was walking quickly, passed his daughter before he saw what she saw: A mother grizzly bear with two cubs.

Before he knew it, the 43-year-old dad felt the bear chomping down on his thigh. Johan wanted to protect his daughter. As the bear was biting him, he at least knew it wasn't going after Jenna. Stuck between the mountain on one side and a steep slope full of prickly bushes on the other, he decided the bushes would be much less painful than the bear's teeth and claws.

Above: A mother bear protecting her cubs will attack if she feels threatened.

As Johan dropped down the slope, the bear turned on Jenna. She tried to use a can of pepper spray, which had fallen out of Johan's pack, but couldn't get the safety clip off. Fur and fangs came at her. She fell backwards over the cliff, striking her head. Johan, assuming the bear was after his daughter, yelled for her to join him on the slope, but instead, the furious mother bear flung itself down on him. He rolled over, and the bear went after his backpack. It probably saved him, but he knew that Jenna didn't have a pack to protect her. Then the bear began to bite the hiker's head. Johan heard the bear's teeth grind on bone—his skull. Not knowing what else to do, he rolled further down the slope to a small ledge. The bear couldn't reach him. It returned to Jenna, who played dead while it bit and jostled her. Finally, sure that its cubs were safe, the bear moved on.

Above: When surprised, grizzly bears become a blur of rage and power.

Both Johan and Jenna survived the attack thanks to the help of hikers, park rangers, helicopter pilots, ambulance drivers, and skilled surgeons and hospital workers, most of whom had never seen such extensive wounds. Johan received 28 deep lacerations, including a ripped-off scalp. A claw had reached in and torn his eye muscle, and he had a fractured neck and five broken vertebrae. Jenna had bite wounds on her shoulder and heel, and a large gash on her cheek. Both realized they were lucky to be alive. Stated Johan, "I was probably one of the most injured people ever to survive something like this."

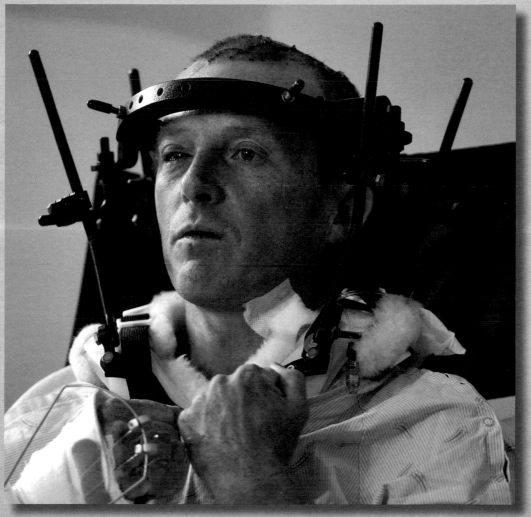

Above: Johan Otter spent weeks in the hospital after the grizzly bear attack.

PANDAS ARE BEARS!

They are adorable, and people love them. Pictures of young pandas being held and bottle-fed by handlers are everywhere. Found only in China, a panda's main diet is bamboo, although wild pandas do eat small mammals and birds.

About the size of a black bear, an adult panda grows to be about 5 to 6 feet (1.5 to 1.8 m) long, and weighs about 150 to 250 pounds (68 to 113 kg). Pandas have short, sharp claws on each paw, and can climb trees easily. Strong muscles power their jaws, allowing them to chew tough plants. Because their food source is available year round, pandas do not hibernate.

Panda attacks are very rare. Most occur in zoos when people decide to get close to the animals for a photo opportunity. Pandas, like all bears, will aggressively defend themselves when they are startled or feel threatened.

Above: Most panda attacks happen in zoos when people get too close.

> "Yang Yang was so cute and I just wanted to cuddle him. I didn't expect he would attack"
>
> —Mr. Liu, November 21, 2008, Qixing Park, Southern China

In 2008, a 21-year-old Chinese student discovered how aggressive pandas can be while on a school trip to Qixing Park in southern China. Mr. Liu climbed a 6.5-foot (2-m) fence, then approached a panda named Yang Yang, who was sleeping. Startled awake, the panda attacked, biting the young man on the arms and legs. The student escaped, and ended his day in the hospital. As he discovered, even though pandas usually move slowly and are cute, they are still fast, powerful wild animals.

Above: Panda bears are cute, but like all bears they possess formidable claws and teeth.

AR BEAR ENCOUNTER

Few people expect to be attacked by a polar bear *inside* a building. However, on a cold November Tuesday in 1993, construction worker Donald L. Chaffin found out that walls and windows do not keep out one of the biggest bears in the world.

A polar bear had been sniffing around a United States Air Force radar base in northern Alaska. The bear probably smelled whale meat that was stored nearby. Twice it came to a ground floor window, and twice workers scared it off. However, the bear returned a third time.

Apparently, the luscious smell of the whale meat was too tempting for this polar bear to pass up. On its third visit, the bear crashed through the window and attacked. Chaffin received the full fury of one of nature's most powerful predators.

Above: A polar bear looking through the window of a pickup truck in Alaska.

Co-workers at the site attempted to scare the bear off by blasting it with fire extinguishers. The thick-skinned bear ignored the cold blasts. Another man, Alexander Polakoff, raced to his room and retrieved an illegally stored shotgun. (All other guns were locked in a cabinet.)

The bear never got his whale meat dinner. Polakoff shot the hungry beast four times, finally killing it.

Broken and bloody, Chaffin was airlifted to a hospital in Anchorage, Alaska. Several hundred stitches later, Donald L. Chaffin was added to the short list of survivors of a polar bear attack.

The United States Air Force added much greater protection to their Arctic facilities. Loaded shotguns and strict procedures have been set up to keep this from happening to anyone else.

Above: A polar bear smells bacon cooking in a kitchen in Churchill, Manitoba, Canada.

Bear attacks are rare. That's one reason why they make the headlines. But what can be done to survive when an attack happens?

First, try not to be attacked! Pay attention to your surroundings. Bears are found near food sources, such as streams and berry patches, as well as dense cover. If you can't see what's ahead because a trail takes a sharp turn, stop and listen before moving ahead. If you're hiking in bear country, talk or sing loudly. Don't surprise the bears. If you encounter a bear cub, leave immediately. The mother is nearby. If you see a dead animal carcass or bear scat, it's possible that a bear is in the area. Bears protect their kills. Get away.

What if you encounter a bear? Don't run. A bear will assume you are prey and attack. Stay standing, and keep your eyes on the bear. If possible, keep a tree or rock between you and the animal. Back up at an angle, but never turn your back on a bear.

Carry pepper spray, and have it ready to use. Sprayed in a bear's eyes or nose, this non-lethal, stinging spray may distract a bear long enough for you to get away.

Right: A bear can sometimes be distracted by pepper spray, giving you time to escape.

Some people climb trees, but black bears can scoot up a tree nearly as fast as a squirrel. You don't want to be stuck up a tree with a bear. Grizzlies don't climb trees, but they move extremely fast. How far can you climb in just a few seconds? That's all the time you'll have.

If you are attacked, fight back. Hit or stab the bear with a rock, a car key, or whatever is in reach to make the bear think that you are dangerous. Only "play dead" if you've come upon a mother bear and her cubs. She is attacking to protect her young, and if she thinks you are no longer a threat, she'll leave. Otherwise, fight back fiercely. You are fighting to save your life.

Above: Sometimes, climbing a tree is your only option, but it's no guarantee of safety.

GLOSSARY

CANINE TEETH

Long, pointed teeth used for biting prey and ripping at meat. Canine teeth are also called fangs.

CARCASS

The dead body of an animal.

INCISORS

Teeth found in the front of the mouth on both top and bottom jaws. Used for cutting or gnawing.

INSTINCT

A way to behave in certain situations that is known, not learned. For example, instinct tells bears to chase running animals, or to attack if they feel threatened.

LACERATION

A deep tear or cut in the skin.

MAULED

To beat or tear at a person or animal, causing extremely serious or deadly physical damage.

MOLARS

Wide, flatter teeth used for grinding up food. Molars are found in the back of the mouth.

Nonretractable Claws

Claws that cannot move back into a paw. Bears have nonretractable claws. Their claws are always out. Cats have retractable claws that move in and out of their paws.

Omnivore

Animals that eat both plants and meat.

Pepper Spray

A canned spray that burns and may sometimes cause temporary blindness, but does not kill.

Play Dead

Unmoving, to pretend to be dead. A survival technique for people attacked by a mother bear protecting her cubs is to play dead.

Predator

An animal that preys on other animals.

Scat

A naturalist's term for animal waste (poop).

Left: Binky, an orphaned wild polar bear at the Alaska Zoo, in Anchorage, Alaska, nearly had an unscheduled lunch when a tourist climbed over two security fences in order to get a close-up of the 1,000-pound (454-kg) bear. Binky grabbed the tourist and began biting her on the leg. After a brief struggle, the tourist was able to wriggle free, leaving Binky with a mouthful of shoe.

INDEX

A grizzly bear catches a fish in the Brooks River in Alaska's Katmai National Park.